Why Animals Hibernate

Cameron Macintosh

Contents

Sleeping in Winter

Winter is the coldest time of the year. It is also a time when some animals cannot find a lot of food to eat.

In winter, many animals hibernate.

When an animal hibernates,
it finds a place that is warm,
and safe from **predators**.
Then, it stays very quiet and still,
or falls into a deep sleep for a long time.

A wood frog hibernates in a gap between two rocks.

When animals hibernate, they do not need to leave their warm places to find food.

Hibernating helps some animals to grow or change, too.

Many insects, frogs, lizards and **mammals** hibernate in winter.

The leopard frog hibernates in a pond.

The hedgehog hibernates to keep warm in winter.

The bearded dragon digs a burrow to hibernate in.

Insects

Antarctic Midge

The Antarctic **midge**
is a tiny insect
that lives in Antarctica.
Antarctica is cold
all year round.

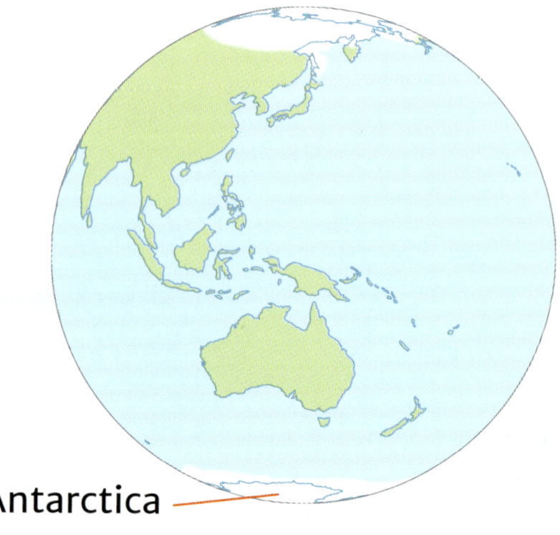

Antarctica is the land around the South Pole.

Before it turns into a midge,
this insect is a grub.
The grub hibernates underneath the ice.
Hibernating helps it to grow.

The Antarctic midge begins life as a grub.

After two years, a fully grown midge comes out from under the ice.
Then, it only lives for about ten more days.

The Antarctic midge looks like a small ant.

Arctic Woolly Bear Moth

The Arctic woolly bear moth is an insect that lives in the Arctic.

Before it turns into a moth, this insect is a caterpillar.

The Arctic is the land and sea around the North Pole.

When it is a caterpillar, the Arctic woolly bear moth has a hairy body.

Each winter, the caterpillar spins silk
to make a thin **cocoon**.
It hibernates inside.

After many winters,
it spins one more cocoon.
This cocoon is very thick.

Finally, a moth comes out of the cocoon.

When the caterpillar has finished growing, it comes out of its woolly cocoon as a moth.

Frogs

Wood Frog

The wood frog lives in forests in North America.

In winter, it is too cold for this frog
to move around to find food.
So, it hibernates under leaves
or among fallen branches.

The frog freezes like ice.
Its heart stops beating and it goes into a deep sleep.

At the end of winter, the wood frog's heart starts beating again.
It begins to look for food.

Leopard Frog

The leopard frog lives near ponds.

In winter, the water in a pond is warmer than the air outside.
So, the leopard frog hibernates underwater, at the bottom of a pond.
While underwater, it breathes through its skin.

A leopard frog hibernates at the bottom of a pond.

At the beginning of spring, the frog comes up to the surface of the pond.

Lizards

Bearded Dragon

The bearded dragon is a lizard that lives in the desert.

During winter, the desert can become very cold. The bearded dragon digs a deep burrow where it hibernates to keep warm.

A bearded dragon digs its burrow.

When winter ends, the bearded dragon comes out of its burrow to find food.

Blue-Tongued Lizard

The blue-tongued lizard lives in grassy places.

It hibernates in winter to stay warm.
It finds a safe place inside a hollow log
or among some rocks.

A blue-tongued lizard looks for a place to hibernate.

If the sun shines in winter,
the lizard comes out to warm up.
Then, it goes back to its safe place to keep hibernating.

When winter ends, the lizard comes out
and looks for food.

Mammals

Hedgehog

The hedgehog lives in grassy fields.

Before winter starts, the hedgehog eats a lot of food. Then, it goes into a burrow to hibernate. It does not need to go looking for food during winter.

A hedgehog hibernates in its burrow.

At the end of winter, the hedgehog comes out of its burrow.
It looks for bugs and grasshoppers to eat.

Brown Bear

The brown bear lives in forests.

In winter, the forests are cold
and there is not a lot of food to be found.

Before winter starts, the brown bear eats
as much food as it can.
Then, it goes into a **den** to hibernate.

During winter, the brown bear stays warm inside its den.
It does not need to go outside to find food.

A brown bear sleeps safe and warm in its den.

If there are other animals nearby, the brown bear can wake up and chase them away.

A hedgehog has made a burrow in some leaves to hibernate in.

Hibernating is an important part of life for many animals.

It helps some animals to stay alive during the cold winter.
It helps other animals to grow and change.

A wood frog hibernates on a leaf.

Glossary

cocoon (*noun*) a silky case made by a caterpillar where it stays safe or grows and changes

den (*noun*) a cave or burrow where a bear sleeps

mammals (*noun*) animals that feed their babies with milk

midge (*noun*) an insect that is like a small ant

predators (*noun*) animals that hunt other animals for food